This spook-tacular book belongs to

....

Peppa Pig™

LADYBIRD BOOKS

UK | USA | Canada | Ireland | Australia | India | New Zealand | South Africa

Ladybird Books is part of the Penguin Random House group of companies
whose addresses can be found at global.penguinrandomhouse.com.

www.penguin.co.uk   www.puffin.co.uk   www.ladybird.co.uk

Penguin
Random House
UK

First published 2020
003

Licensed by
Hasbro   **eOne**

Printed in China

The authorized representative in the EEA is Penguin Random House Ireland,
Morrison Chambers, 32 Nassau Street, Dublin D02 YH68

A CIP catalogue record for this book is available from the British Library

ISBN: 978-0-241-41226-8

All correspondence to:
Ladybird Books, Penguin Random House Children's
One Embassy Gardens, 8 Viaduct Gardens, London SW11 7BW

FSC
www.fsc.org

MIX
Paper from
responsible sources
FSC® C018179

BEWARE!
LOW
FLYING
BATS

Peppa's Spooky Halloween

It was Halloween, and Peppa and George were at Granny and Grandpa Pig's house. "Please can we only do spooky things today, Granny?" asked Peppa.

"Yes, of course," replied Granny Pig.
"Most definitely!" added Grandpa Pig.
Grandpa Pig loves Halloween!

"Don't these cakes look yummy?" said Grandpa Pig.
"They're not yummy, Grandpa," said Peppa.
"They're spooky!"
"Oh, yes. **Very** spooky!"
Grandpa Pig grinned.

"Your house isn't very spooky, Grandpa," said Peppa.
"It isn't at the moment . . ." said Grandpa Pig, showing Peppa a great big box, "but let's see what we can do with these decorations."

"Wow!" gasped Peppa. "You have so many Halloween decorations!"
"Yes," said Grandpa Pig. "We've collected a lot over the years."

Hee! Hee!

"Monsta-ROAR!" shouted George, putting on a funny monster costume.

"Look at me! Heh! Heh! Heeh!" cackled Peppa, who was dressed as a witch.

Hee! Hee!

"And I am zee spoookeeee vampire. Ha! Ha!" said Grandpa Pig in his best vampire voice.

Hee! Hee!

"Let's try on **all** the spooky costumes!" cried Peppa excitedly.

"Mum-eee!" shouted George, dressing up as a mummy and falling over his bandages.

BEWARE!
LOW
FLYING
BATS

"Miaow!" purred Peppa, looking just like a witch's cat.

"Tic-kal! Tic-kal!" said George, tickling Grandpa Pig with one of his eight furry spider's legs.

"I'm rrrr-attling my b-b-bones . . ." said Peppa, shaking her arms and legs in a skeleton costume.

ressed up as ghosts!

"**BOO!**" shouted Peppa, jumping in front of Granny Pig.
"Ooh, you scared me, Ghost George!" said Granny Pig.

"No, I'm Ghost Peppa, Granny.
That's Ghost George over there!"
said Peppa, pointing and giggling.

Hee!
Hee!

Peppa and George decided to change one more time. George liked the skeleton costume the best, but Peppa had something else in mind.

"Look at me!" said Peppa.
"I'm a Magical Halloween Unicorn!"

"Well, we can't have Halloween without a Magical Halloween Unicorn, can we?" laughed Grandpa Pig.

Granny and Grandpa Pig gave Peppa and George a big round of applause. "You're both so spooky!" said Granny Pig.

"Yes!" cried Peppa. "We can invite Mummy and Daddy and our friends to watch it!"

"That sounds like lots of fun!" said Granny Pig.

"Spooky fun?" asked Peppa.

"Oh yes, of course, Peppa. Spooky fun," said Granny Pig, laughing.

CAUTION!
MONSTERS
CROSSING

The door creaked open, and there stood
Grandpa Pig in his costume. "Velcome to zee
Spooky House," he said. "I trust you have
come to vatch zis evening's performance of
zee Spooky Show?"
"Er, yes?" replied Daddy Pig, a little confused.

Eeeekk!

Once all their friends had arrived . . .
"It's time for the Spooky Show!" announced Peppa.
"We hope you find it –"

"Spoooo-keee!" cried George.
Everyone in the audience clapped and cheered excitedly.

Peppa and George took it in turns to dress up in the spooky costumes, jump in front of the audience and shout "BOO!"

George was a monster . . .

and a mummy . . .

and a furry spider.

And Peppa was
a black cat . . .

a rattly
skeleton . . .

a ghost . . .

Hee!

Hee!

and a cackling witch!

"Oooh!" gasped their friends, giggling.
"Soooo spooky!"

At the end of the show, Peppa and George jumped out in their favourite costumes.
"I am the Magical Halloween Unicorn, and this is Skeleton George!" Peppa cried. "We hope you enjoyed our show."

Peppa and George bowed as the audience clapped.
"*Awoooo!*" cheered Danny Dog in his werewolf costume.

AWOOoo!

"Now then, everyone," said Granny Pig,
"It's time for some spooky dancing!"
"Hooray!" everybody cheered, jumping
up to dance to the funny spooky music.

"Did you have a fun day at Granny and Grandpa's house?"
Mummy Pig asked Peppa and George on their way home.
"No, Mummy, it wasn't fun," replied Peppa.
"It was spook-tacular!"

Mwah!
Ha! Ha!

CAUTION!

MONSTERS
CROSSING

Peppa and George love Halloween.
Everyone loves Halloween!